I0677719

Wakefield Press

The Rocks Remain

Blak Poetry and Story

The Rocks Remain

Blak Poetry and Story

Edited by
Karen Wyld and Dominic Guerrera

With contributions from
Noah Amundson, Ben Armstrong, Nancy Bates,
Edoardo Crismani, Brad Darkson, Ali Cobby Eckermann,
Kathryn Gledhill-Tucker, Dominic Guerrera, Natalie Harkin,
Sheena Hayes, Lulu Houdini, Michael Larkin, Tabitha Lean,
Angie Faye Martin, Steven Pappin, Dylan Peisley, Taryn Poole,
Sonya Rankine, Shania Richards, Brooke Scobie, Rick Slager,
Barrina South, Jayda Wilson, Karen Wyld

**Wakefield
Press**

Wakefield Press
16 Rose Street
Mile End
South Australia 5031
www.wakefieldpress.com.au

First published 2024

Edited by Angie Faye Martin
Cover designed by Rachel Harris, Bit Scribbly Design
Cover artwork by James Tylor
Designed and typeset by Clinton Ellicott, Wakefield Press

This project has been assisted by the Australian Government through
Creative Australia, its arts funding and advisory body.

ISBN 978 1 92304 238 4

NATIONAL
LIBRARY
OF AUSTRALIA
A catalogue record for this
book is available from the
National Library of Australia

CORIOLE
McLAREN VALE
Wakefield Press thanks
Coriole Vineyards for
continued support

Contents

A Word from the Editors

There was some serendipity behind the creation of this anthology: as if it had a life of its own, beyond our vision, and just needed a little bit of help from us to bring it into reality.

In undertaking this project, our main aims were to nurture and showcase new, emerging and established First Nations writers and poets who have connections to South Australia; while also not allowing notions of borders to engender exclusions. And we were interested in seeing what would emerge if we didn't dictate themes, genres, or narrative forms: we were pleasantly surprised.

The image on the front cover is titled *Wirramumiyu* (2017), from James Tylor's *Turalayinthi Yarta* collection. Turalayinthi Yarta is a Kaurna Miyurna phrase that means 'to see yourself in the landscape' – a concept we feel is reflected in this anthology.

The title of this anthology comes from Brad Darkson's prose piece, 'waiting for kakirra':

> Ignore the present. Forget the past. The rocks remain unmoved.
> Waiting, as kakirra passes overhead.

Many of the selected works feature rocks, or elements of rock. The title was waiting for us to notice it. But why rocks? Because they remain – unmoved. Always have, and always will.

Rock is Country. It's our home and our kin. Bedrock.

Rock is resistance, and survival. Rock is staunchly sovereign.

Like all carbon-based lifeforms, rocks contain tiny fragments of stardust. Just like us.

Rocks are much more than minerals. They can be precious gemstones, or hold fossilised remnants of creatures that no longer walk this earth.

Our Elders, family, cultures, law and lores are our rocks. Anchors to remind us what's really important, and what our responsibilities are for each other and Country.

Some rocks are ancestral beings. Their stories are told from generation to generation, teaching and reminding. Other stories are held close; secret-sacred, between rock and a select few.

Some rocks are stubborn, unmoveable, determined. Still here.

Chip away at rock, gather the stones – they make good weapons and tools.

Rocks can be used to grind the seeds and grains to make the damper that nourishes our families. Rocks were used to make the hunting tools that our hands still remember.

Rocks protect us. They can be used for shelter, or for building blocks.

Wind kisses rock. Water caresses it. And still the rocks remain. Always.

When you touch a rock – can you feel the essence of those who've travelled before you? Rocks hold thoughts, emotions, and story.

In these pages there are many types of rocks. Lovers, teachers, nurturers and friends. Resistance fighters, protectors and providers. The rocks appear subtly, or are central to the story.

Find the rocks within these pages. Listen. *What story do they hold for you?*

Acknowledgements

This anthology was produced and partially written on Kaurna Yarta. We respect Kaurna people's continuous connections to land, seas and skies, and acknowledge Kaurna Elders past and present.

Through this book, we wish to honour literary Elders who came before us, creating pathways for us to travel more easily. We remember published Nunga poets, writers and illustrators who have passed on, including: David Unaipon, Margaret Brusnahan, Doreen Kartinyeri, Doris Kartinyeri, Veronica Brodie, Ruby Hunter, Ian Abdulla, Yami Lester, Buck McKenzie, Georgina Williams and Vince Copley. And renowned Nunga authors who are nurturing new poets and writers in South Australia: Uncle Lewis O'Brien, Ali Cobby Eckermann, Natalie Harkin and Dylan Coleman.

We acknowledge the many people who made this anthology possible. Such as Michael Bollen and team at Wakefield Press for supporting our vision to nurture Blak writers in South Australia, and producing this book. Thanks to Angie Faye Martin from Versed Writings for her expert copyediting; we valued the support of an Aboriginal editor to help shape this collection.

We thank Brad Darkson for the prose that inspired the book's title. And James Tylor, who allowed use of his artwork for the front cover.

We're grateful to Creative Australia for the project funding. Also Writers SA for their ongoing support and contribution to the ecology of Aboriginal writers in South Australia, particularly Jessica Alice and Bronwyn Tilley. We are proud members of our local South Australia First Nation Writers Group and want to acknowledge Edoardo Crismani and the members – local Blak writers groups are essential to build up local Blak writers.

We thank our families, friends, and mentors for their support and generosity.

We acknowledge the idea of a South Australian based anthology of Aboriginal writers was not ours alone, but rather something that has been spoken about over a few years. And we're thankful that Michael Bollen at Wakefield Press readily agreed to our proposal for this book.

Thank you to the poets and writers that contributed to this anthology, trusting us with their stories. Poems and prose that connected together so well – it would appear these rocks (aka stories) had been waiting for us.

We have used the spelling Blak in the title on purpose, as have some of the writers in their own work. In the 1990s, Destiny Deacon, a Kua Kua and Erub/Mer artist, coined the term Blak to reject the white gaze on their work. It's now used by some Aboriginal and Torres Strait Islander people as a political statement, and to reassert identity.

Nukkinya
Dominic and Karen

waiting for kakirra

Brad Darkson

in consultation with Ngangki Burka Senior Kaurna woman
Aunty Lynette Crocker

One person picks up a rock with the help of another and places it down in a circular formation, a cool sensation up to the knee, waiting for the tide ...

How did we get here? Rewind to the beginning.

Munaintyarlu – curl up that sea, on the crest of a wave. Creation is in the now.

Kakirra the Moon physically pulls the ocean upwards as she passes overhead in a planetary collaboration. Saltwater moves against rock, slowly eroding minerals to form our oceans. Yarta, the Earth, inhales. Oceans rise. An ancient fault line slowly folds a layer of rock over an eternity. Glacial mudstone deposited from a time defined by cold, formed through eons of immense pressure and elevated temperature. Exhale as oceans recede.

Fungi digest rocks to provide soil for plants. Bacteria provide oxygen to create atmosphere. Each new multi-species community assembled in the process of collaborative world-making and survival.

Tending. Listening to Country. Kaurna bring kardla fire to yarta, collaborating with grasslands, trees and other living things that overlap in these ecologies. Kakirra the Moon passes overhead.

Kauwi water rises to the heat. The silence of young shoots underfoot. Freshwater drains from deep rooted grasslands into a gently flowing stream, yawning to meet saltwater, and new collaborations take place. Ceremony. Sing to the ocean. A spring nearby guides the path of the stones into a circular formation. World-making continues.

Enter the economy > oeconomia > oikonomia > oikos (house) + nemein (manage). Ideas of progress and looking to a better future for humanity. One full of promise and ease powered by economic advancement and capital. Humans external to the environment.

Industrial progress. Move forward. Forget the present. Kakirra passes overhead.

Humanist and rationalist ideas that centre science and reason over the spiritual and the non-human place emphasis on the individual – consciousness, agency. Our attention drifts further from the collaborative nature of survival in world-making. Survival becomes about the individual. The human species in a growth economy. Humans external to the environment. A new identity of place formed through modernity and progress and ownership of Country. Enormous rock structures take the place of small ones for the sake of profit.

Ignore the present. Forget the past. The rocks remain unmoved. Waiting, as kakirra passes overhead.

Today we ask ourselves what led us to the precipice of ecological catastrophe. Still we push on. Forward. Disconnected from the present. Searching for technological collaborations that might extend our survival in the wreckage of a global economy. A virtual ghost of a time that was present and now past.

One person picks up a rock with the help of another and places it down in a circular formation, a cool sensation up to the knee, waiting for kakirra.

Daring not to Dream
Michael Larkin

As the monotones of mountain grey
Enclose what could have been,
We scratch against the granite
At one hundred words per minute,
Descending into charcoal pits
To chip away our captive minds,
Pin our hopes to silent walls,
Surrender to the stone.

We scratch against the granite
At one hundred words per minute,
Grounded in survival's course
We grip against the sliding slopes,
Pin our hopes to silent walls,
Surrender to the stone,
Daring not to dream, outside the knowing day,
And yet again another day.

Grounded in survival's course
We grip against the sliding slopes,
Without rebirth or reconnection,
Transcendence buried under clay,
Daring not to dream, outside the knowing day,
And yet again another day,
In solemn herds we hold the strain,
Mourn for those we can't regain.

Without rebirth or reconnection,
Transcendence buried under clay,
Descending into charcoal pits,
To chip away our captive minds,
In solemn herds we hold the strain,
Mourn for those we can't regain,
As the monotones of mountain grey
Enclose what could have been.

Away from Country
Steven Pappin

My language and my country are parts of me

Wiimpatya palku-tya ngapa – Paakantyi palku
    I can speak my Aboriginal language – Barkindji Language

Ngapa, pari-mala; para-miri, para-kiira
    I, walked away, to a far away place, a distant land

Yartu ngiintalana
    The wind is blowing

Kiira-kali yanalathika
    Country is always calling me to return

Thalt-intu-ayi!
    You listen to me!

Kiiki-ili-nu, yapara-ayi. ngiingka-taapa
    This is my camp, right here now. I shall stay

Kila yanmaltaapa
    I won't cry (I won't be sorry)

Panypakana ngiingka-apa
    I am sitting in the sunshine

Yamirina ngukuna wirkataapa
 I shall swim in the shallow water

Wimpaty-uku-ngaatha, kiira-ngaatha
 Without a lot of people, without Country

Yungaaku
 Alone

Home within me
Angie Faye Martin

The roots of the towering gum reach into the muddy brown waters
    Where I lay, floating
I feel the soft flow around
    my body,
    my skin; holding me.
I smell the eucalyptus oils in the air and bring them deep into my lungs.

The leaves flicker high above, their green-grey hues dance
    with a clear blue sky,
Their backdrop.

The stars, planets and all the world and time is up there
And around me.

I am here.
    One with Country.
        With my ancestors – the beauty and peace of my present,
    I let the waters carry me into a future,
        Knowing Country is with me.
            It will never let me go.
            I am one with it. It is one with me. We are the same.
            Never ending, and never beginning.

Vermin-Proof Fence
Rick Slager

Luke idled along in his ute, patrolling the boundary fence. Pasture on his side, dense scrub on the other. Watching and waiting for the approaching front, he steered with his knees to free up his hands to roll a ciggy. His UHF radio crackled with voices swinging between blame, panic, humour and despair, depending on their vicinity to danger and loss.

> '... *where's the help from the government?'*
> '... *getting away from us ...'*
> '... *need pumps and radios ...'*
> '... *no one's ever seen it like this ...'*
> '... *throwing resources at us if we were Abos ...'*

Popping the ute out of gear and rolling to a stop, Luke sat for a moment and sparked his ciggy to life, drawing deeply. He exhaled a plume of blue smoke, then hopped out to check the fuel level in the pump and water in the tank on the tray for what felt like the hundredth time that day, as he had done every day over the past two weeks. He'd thought stepping up and volunteering would be about saving lives; stopping the advance of the front, protecting towns, saving his Country. It wasn't like that at all.

To the north and west the billowing cloud of smoke reached high into the atmosphere. It was growing in intensity with the heat, filtering the light and tainting the day sepia. The smoke looked like how he imagined a cyclonic storm would, except for the different hues: black, white, brown, depending on what was burning. An increasingly hot, gusty wind relentlessly rolled across the bush, dropping ash, burnt gum leaves and embers like a filthy black snow.

A spot fire burst to life in the dry pasture he was patrolling. He pushed up the throttle of his pump and jumped back in his old ute. Adrenaline spiked his heart rate as he raced, bumping across the hundred metres of dry pasture, putting himself in front of the fire's path. Opening the nozzle of his water hose he doused the flames before it could get into the heavily vegetated bank on the far side of the paddock.

Luke's elevated heart rate escalated his headache which he'd had for more than a week from breathing in too much smoke – it throbbed behind his eyes. Pushing up his goggles, he spat the sodden cigarette butt out of his mouth and squeezed his eyes closed, pushing them with his filthy, burnt fingers, rubbing ash, dirt and sweat stinging into his eyes.

'... *getting away from us ...*'
'*Haha, what are ya doing ...*'
'... *it's all gone.*'

When Luke first ventured out to fight the fires he naively assumed a disaster like this would bring the community together, the whole community. *Us versus the destruction of everything we hold dear.* It wasn't like that at all. The same old sides existed now as they did before. It shocked him that protecting farmers' boundary fences was the main objective. Houses, sheds, machinery, stock and pasture also had varying importance but not necessarily in that order. You'd be laughed at if you mentioned protecting the bush and the native animals that lived in it. People saw the natural environment as the cause not something that needed protecting.

Stock made money but could be moved or covered by insurance. Pasture fed the stock but if it burnt it would regrow and the stock could be fed hay. Boundary fences kept the stock in the paddocks and native animals off the pasture. Any grass the native animals ate was energy that could have been converted into growth of the stock and therefore money. Without a functioning boundary fence a farm could not make money. Rebuilding it after a fire was a massively time-consuming job (if the materials could even be found in a post-fire market when everyone would be after them).

Luke let the nozzle of his hose dribble cool water over his burnt hand. The pain from the blisters, now burst, was unrelenting. He had picked up a twisted steel star-dropper from the remains of a destroyed fence to avoid anyone puncturing a tyre, but it was hot from laying on the smouldering ground. The pain brought unwanted memories of patrolling other fence lines during the fires. Things he now dreamt about, things he knew he'd never forget and would have to witness again. Guilt bubbled up in his chest.

He got back in the ute and attempted to roll another durrie but the paper tore apart in his wet fingers. Flicking away the soggy mess he resumed his crawling patrol, looking for spot fires, trying not to think about what was coming. It didn't work. The radio continued with its constant chatter:

'... *fucking national parks* ...'

'... *what were they thinking?*'

'... *a lot to answer for* ...'

Some of the shame he felt was justified but other ideas he knew were complex and unwarranted. The farmers blamed the national parks for not maintaining their fire breaks or acting quick enough when the fires started. But the farmers neglected any land under their control that wasn't arable. And then there was the changing climate. Warming up. Getting drier.

But isn't all this Country really my people's responsibility? He knew they had been shut out of the land since colonisation by the farmer's fences.

17

Unable to perform the ceremonies and caring burns that Country needed to maintain its health. *So it's not really my fault, is it?* And Luke's family had assimilated early, only now was he learning and reconnecting. Yet because of this he felt his ancestors watching. Waiting.

Picking up his phone to check for coverage, the screen showed a thermometer and read, 'Temperature. Phone needs to cool down before you can use it.' *That's not going to happen.* There hadn't been any phone reception for a week anyway, but Luke kept checking, wanting to call his neighbour. He was worried about his dog, Millie, his best mate, shut up in his rented house back in town. He hadn't seen her for days because he'd been camping out to fight the fires, protecting farmers' fences.

He looked to the southeast, back toward town. The plumes of smoke were so big it made it impossible to guess how close the numerous fronts were to the town. He was almost glad his phone wasn't working so he couldn't look at his socials. The information he did get came from word-of-mouth or the ABC radio and was incomplete, out-of-date or plain wrong. Someone he randomly bumped into handing out cold toasted egg and bacon sandwiches and just out-of-date iced coffee swore the town would never be allowed to burn; last refuge, vital infrastructure and whatever. Then yesterday he'd heard on the UHF radio that the pub and the school were gone, sending terror lancing through his heart, but the story turned out to be bullshit anyway.

Another spot fire started up on the other side of the dam – he almost didn't see it in time because the light was beginning to fail due to the increasing thickness and ceaseless approach of the main smoke cloud. When he did notice the flames he jumped out to turn up the revs of his pump, clambered back in and gunned the ute over to put it out.

In the end, the bare earth of the dam wall gave him the chance to get it under control as it starved the building fire of fuel.

Turning the pump back down to an idle, Luke dried his shaky hands and rolled and lit a smoke. In the relative quiet he thought he heard the sound he'd been dreading but expecting. He killed the pump and listened. Sure enough, he could clearly hear the roar of the front now. His heart rate began to ratchet up again.

'Luke. Are ya there?' The radio jolted his awareness back to the ute.

Fumbling with the radio he pushed the button and responded, 'Yeah, Luke here. What's going on?' He didn't know who was on the other end and it didn't much matter.

'Are you ok over there? Has it got to that fence line yet?' The disembodied voice asked.

'Not yet but I don't reckon it's far off.' Luke let go of the button. Pressed it again, 'Hard to tell though.'

'We're busy over on the north-eastern boundary.' Luke had no idea where they were talking about. 'You'll be all right over there won't you?'

Who the fuck knows. 'Yeah. I'm alright.'

'Let us know if you need a hand mate.'

'Ok.' If Luke had learnt anything over the last two weeks, and he'd learnt a lot, by the time he realised he needed help it was generally too late. But what could he say? The fire had rolled over everything that might have stopped a normal fire; bulldozed breaks, roads and creeks; first the CFS and then the farm units fleeing before it. *But you had to try …?*

As Luke pulled the rip cord, bringing the pump back to life, and pushed the throttle up to its maximum noise, the smoke started rolling through at ground level, so thick that his eyes and nose were streaming with tears and snot. He jumped back in the ute, pulled down his goggles and tried to clean them, smearing more sweat and ash across the gritty lenses. Pulling up his filthy dust mask from under his chin, he vowed he'd steal better ones out of the next CFS truck he came across, even though he hadn't seen one for a couple of days. They were a weak attempt at keeping the smoke out of his eyes and lungs but it was all he could do to prepare himself to protect the fence from the now imminent front.

Luke's anxiety was building with the roar of the fire. He made the decision to abandon monitoring the spot fires in the pasture and let it burn. He started a slow drive up and down the boundary fence peering through the smoke into the scrub on the other side. It wasn't long before he started to see the orange and red flickers of flame through the darkness of the dense bush and hear the crackle and pop of drought-dry eucalypt igniting over the general howl of the encroaching inferno.

It was the moment he'd been dreading. At first it was the birds, landing on the fence and in the branches of the trees on the edge of the scrub, fleeing the fire, fighting their natural instinct to stay in the cover of bush. An owl, feathers aflame, flew and crashed into the tree canopy just over the fence. The guilt surged in his gut, up his throat, like ash on his tongue. In ones and twos, and then in dozens, came the wallabies, kangaroos, possums, echidnas, bandicoots, goannas, koalas and everyone else. Racing away from their usual refuges in the scrub toward the relative safety of the open pasture only to run headlong into the vermin-proof fence. The chest-high, ring-lock wire fence with chicken wire covering the bottom half and topped by double strands of barbed wire, held up by pine posts, was built specifically to keep out all but the bravest kangaroo – kangaroos willing to risk a bullet for the farmers' precious pasture. The vermin-proof fence Luke was responsible for protecting was identical to so many he had protected and some he'd lost over the past two weeks. At every fence line he'd witnessed and enabled similar events as he watched them unfold before him.

Animals bolted up and down the fence mirroring Luke's slow patrol on the opposite side as they looked for an escape from the burning bush, choked with decades of neglect. The fire was so close now that some fence posts were igniting from the radiant heat, even though the flames were metres away over the bare ground of the break, so Luke started to methodically hose them down one after another. The animals were bashing into, and tumbling over, each other in their panic, with the odd quietness of native animals, nothing more than their odd rasping calls to voice the pain of burning fur and flesh.

A huge buck kangaroo came bounding out of the burning scrub, more than half-blind with pain, making for the open pasture. He missed the jump, tumbling over the barbed wire in a mess of ripped flesh, burnt fur and ash. He picked himself up and continued on his mad dash into burnt, hot but relatively safe open pasture. As Luke turned back to the fence the whole scrub line was ablaze. He saw a koala in a sugar gum deceptively calm, attempting to remove the fire from its body but only managing to scrape away the burnt hair and skin revealing the pink and black flesh beneath. He raced along, his ute revving too high between fence posts, not changing out of first gear so it wouldn't stall as he slowed every ten metres to douse the flames eating each pine post. Not having a mate on the back of his ute to hold the hose, Luke could only fight the fire out of the driver's side window. So at the end of each run along the fence he turned around and gunned it back to the beginning to start the process again.

Luke tried to saturate the animals at each post but he knew he was running out of water and the farmers would be angry with him for wasting time and water on them when it meant fence posts burning. The tone of the pump changed and the water spluttered out. He was empty. Luke jumped out of the ute, turned off the pump so it didn't overheat from running dry, got back in and raced across the three hundred metres of smouldering grass to the dam to refill.

Luke took the time waiting for the tank to fill to tell the others over the UHF that the fire was at the fence line and he needed help. He screamed it into the chaos of voices on the radio but it was a waste of time. Everyone was fighting their own battles as the fire swarmed all the farms in the area. The UHF was awash with panic. Men yelling over each other, breaking each other's sentences into gibberish with their own calls for help, requests of what to do, asking where the fire was, men crying.

The water tank filled and Luke raced back to the fence and found animals piled up against it, a writhing mound of pain, hundreds of metres long. The intensity of the front had peaked, all the leaves of the eucalypts and the grasses and understorey were on fire. All the flammable material around the base of the fence posts had burnt away so the ones that were left would probably endure if he kept dousing them one after another. The animals wouldn't.

Luke thought of Millie waiting for him at home. He looked at the animals that his people had lived beside forever, who, no matter how he looked at it, he had an obligation to care for. He looked at the pasture still burning in spots, carrying the fire towards the bush lining the creek on the other side of the paddock. Another paddock closer to town and his dog.

These people he was helping saw no value, held no respect for the bush or the native animals that lived on their land. Holding the land, making fortunes from its desecration had to mean they held responsibility for it. Not just the arable acres and domesticated animals and plants. All of it. They need to share the land with the other animals, not treat them as vermin or the non-arable acres as wasteland. Everyone must hold responsibility. *We can't let this keep happening.*

Luke made up his mind. He chose a side. Rolling to a stop, he got out and picked up a pair of pliers out of the tray of the ute. Wishing he had done it the first time and knowing this would probably be the last time he'd get the chance, because he'd never be trusted to protect one again, but also knowing his ancestors stood beside him; he cut the vermin-proof fence.

Shielding his face from the intense heat, he tripped on the desperate animals streaming around him and fell to the hot ground. He crawled out of reach of the flames and stumbled to his ute, blind from the tears and smoke, nose streaming with snot and unable to take a deep breath. He leaned on his ute ripping off his mask, vomited and cried.

When Luke could see again and breathe a little easier he washed the vomit from his face and shirt with the fire hose, climbed back into the ute and cruised the vermin-proof fence one more time. Ignoring the posts now fully ablaze he stopped to cut it every twenty-five metres or so, letting the animals that were still capable of moving escape into the open pasture.

His eyes and nose were running so much when the farmer found him he didn't realise Luke was crying. He was spraying down burnt animals with water if they didn't run away and clubbing those that were too burnt to survive with a hardwood club he usually used to dispatch animals that tourists hit with their cars and left floundering on the roads.

'What the fuck are you doing wasting time here? That fence is fucked. I'm going to help the Smiths over on Rifle Range Road,' the farmer yelled before tearing off across the paddock.

Luke stood with a dead koala at his feet, waddy covered in both blood from the animals and from his burn-wounded hand hanging at his side. He stared at the dozens of animals on the burnt paddock standing in little groups. It was odd seeing them out in the open during the day, even in this madness. Many of them were alive. Almost all were burnt to varying degrees. Some without feet or eyes. Too many injured beyond hope of recovery and suffering in their last agonising hours of life for Luke to put them out of their misery, and too few people capable or willing to give enough of a shit to help.

Luke chucked the waddy in the tray of the ute and flicked the kill switch on the pump, cutting its endless noise. He got in the cab and drove slowly across the paddock to the gate, then turned onto the gravel road, toward town and his dog Millie.

Cockatoos
Barrina South

my eyes caress his limbs
diaphanous droplets
glisten like a crown on the canopy

I press against the cool bark

from the valley floor
whee-la whee-la

                                             whee-la

a mournful cry that has
circled all day
bringing more makarra

some land heavy
loosen the jewels
that shower down
onto the nape of my neck

others crack pine cones

a glimpse of a yellow blush cheek
I eavesdrop on clicks and chatter
envious of their gentle allopreening

as they leave
believing I can touch their sombre underbellies
reach out

                                        I am home

unwelcome to country
Dominic Guerrera

thank you for gathering unlawfully on my land
it's often said that as Aboriginal people we live within two worlds
    this is not true
we live in a state of colonisation
i was invited by a white person to come here today
and welcome you to my country
but that won't be happening
because to be frank
you're not welcome

you have overstayed your self-imposed welcome
and we are fed up with you
    your colony
        and your destructive murdering ways
we have had enough, it's gone on for too long
that even the earth is rejecting you

if our lives matter
    and they do
then your presence is no longer needed
because no matter what scenario of reconciliation
or cohabitation that is proposed
we are the ones who are always paying the heavy cost
and usually it's with our lives

if we all bleed the same colour
then why are we always the ones bleeding?

how about instead of country, we welcome you
the poverty and the disparity of wealth
the instability that echo through our daily lives because of your
    disruption
i wholeheartedly welcome you to dying 10 years younger
or   trying on a spit-hood
suffocating
as police cuff and slide you into a paddy-hearse

please feel welcome to all the diseases, infections, chronic illnesses,
    disabilities and injuries
brought on by your racism
not because of our race
they are here
waiting for you
come collect them

acknowledge the privileges of being able to gather in public spaces,
uninterrupted by the colony or its forces
because when white people drink in parklands they call it a festival
but when Aboriginal people drink in parklands, they call the cops

the disruption of our gatherings is a deliberate attempt to sever our
    connection to land and with each other

it's time to bring forth a future that doesn't centre this continent on
    white lies
where Aboriginal lives are valued and celebrated
where we can live full and healthy lives
but until then,
            consider yourself unwelcome to country

you cut off my native tongue and here I am sewing it back on
Jayda Wilson

slightly bruised
a mouth full of stitches

my words soften
in hopes that the tongue you cut off
regains
reclaims
and heals

for when speaking my tongue, now reborn
shall these words I speak
cut
  you
  deep

Slightly ngarndarn
ira stitches-muga

ngadyu wangga dyula
in hopes that dyarling nyubuli dyaniga-nda
regains
reclaims
and heals

ngadyu wangga wanggarn, idha-birna
nhaladhaga wangga ngadhu wangga-nda
nyubuli
  ganinyara
  dhargal

This translation is purely an act as a means of translating and does not capture how it would be traditionally used.

Spirit Gate
Ali Cobby Eckerman

It was pitch black when Trevor woke. He couldn't remember where
he was at first; he couldn't remember falling asleep. He had planned
to meet some mates down at the pub for the weekly pool comp, but
figured that was all over now. Something seemed odd. He didn't move,
although his eyes darted left and right across the room. Slowly the
voice of his tjamu became the only sound he could hear, not his gentle
voice but strong chanting, repeating the same words over and over.
Trevor froze; he hadn't heard this Song in a long time, and always
in a whisper. Promptly he rose from the lounge and began chucking
clothes in a knapsack. He lifted a battered tin from the back of the
wardrobe. Opening the lid he stared at the contents. Trevor closed his
eyes a while before placing the box in his pack.

The 671 direct flight from Melbourne to Alice Springs left at 11.05 on
a bleak overcast morning. Trevor grimaced when he was allocated a B
seat; it was too late to change, as the plane was full. He was squashed
between a man in a suit and a young woman with blonde hair who
chattered non-stop as passengers stowed their luggage and took their
seats. Trevor mumbled polite replies; he was reluctant talking to
tourists about central Australia. For once he was glad his complexion
hid his Aboriginality; his blue eyes, ginger hair and freckles had been
inherited from his Irish grandfather, who he had never met. As the
plane taxied to the runway Trevor shut his eyes. He hated this part of
the flight the most; he could not relax during take-off. Thankfully, the
woman stopped talking.

Once in the air Rebecca, *call me Beck*, set up her laptop. He watched
through squinted eyes as her fingers flew over the keyboard. His
interest rose when she replayed an interview with an old Aboriginal
man in a wheelchair. He recognised the Hetti Perkins Aged Care decor

in the background and strained his ears to listen to the recorded conversation.

'Me be gone soon, gone from this place,' menaced the old man from his chair. The video showed a hand holding the microphone closer to him, seemingly wanting to capture his every word. 'No-one gonna know for one day, might be one week,' he began to cackle. 'No-one gonna know till we all gone.'

'What does that mean?' a frantic voice asked impatiently and loudly. But she was too late, the old man was lost in his own soft laughter. A nurse came and wheeled him away. The screen went blank. Beck played the video several times, making comments on a small hand-held recorder. She seemed engrossed until, noticing Trevor's interest, quickly closed her laptop.

Trevor had first heard about the disappearances on the news late last night. He couldn't recall how long he sat staring at the screen in disbelief, before jumping off the couch to get to the phone. He rang his tjamu's phone at the Number Six Town Camp but it rang out. Trevor redialled the number several times before giving up. Funny thing that old man was always home from town by sunset, to avoid the humbug from family members, which seemed to increase in the twilight hours.

Returning to the couch, Trevor had allowed his mind to wander to his tjamu's house. Everyone knew the old man spent his nights sitting quietly with his dogs next to a smoky fire. Trevor liked to join his tjamu around the fire and wait for conversation. Last time Tjamu told him this is the best time of the day when he can talk to Nana. She had passed away suddenly last year and Tjamu missed her terribly. Trevor could see the loss in his tjamu's eyes, and the limp in his footsteps let everyone know a bit of him had died with her.

After collecting his luggage from the carousel, Trevor stood in the sunshine outside the airport and waited for a taxi. He saw Beck climb into a 4WD with the ABC Radio logo painted on the side. He waved as the car drove past but she was too busy talking to the driver to notice him. A taxi raced to a halt before him and climbing inside, Trevor asked to be driven the 15 kilometres into town. Trevor was quiet, enjoying the colour of desert ochres embedded in the landscape along the route, framed by the soft pastel blue of the sacred mountain ranges. He glanced across at the town camp as they sped past the old drive-in site. The road was deserted. Usually groups of people rested under the old gum trees, watching out for family members who were back in town, waiting for anything unusual or exciting. Tears sprung to Trevor's eyes as they drove through the gap, the entrance into town where the dry riverbed cut a defined break between the ranges. It is always emotional to return to his place of birth.

The cabbie noticed his silence and wandering eyes. 'You another reporter?' The question hung between them. Trevor refused to comment. 'You must be wondering where they all gone to? It's a bloody joke really! Fucked up the local economy they did, after all we invested in this town. Always were ungrateful bastards.'

Trevor stared ahead. Through the gap the road was uninhabited. It was surreal that absolutely no Aboriginal people were on the streets. An odd feeling seemed to emanate from the avenue of gum trees. Trevor felt the taxi driver's eyes staring at him through the rear vision mirror, so he tried to keep his face blank. Progress Medical Centre looked derelict as the gates hung open on broken hinges. The hospital car park was empty of people and cars. Even the Municipal lawns were empty of any people. Trevor paid the fare and climbed out of the cab without saying a word.

After standing at the top end of the mall for several minutes Trevor slowly walked to Bar Doppios. It was one of the few remaining cafes open for business in town. The place buzzed with the conversations of clientele: artists, social and youth workers, hippie-types, and government 'yuppie' experts gathered together sipping coffee, trying to solve the mystery. Trevor sat alone, eavesdropping. He avoided the few glances his way, keeping his head down.

Snippets of conversation confirmed that all Aboriginal people had vacated the township region about one week ago. There had been no warning of the exile, no specific signs to the exodus, and most people had failed to notice the blackfellas had left in entirety for several days. People had just assumed they'd gone for another funeral, or a football carnival, or collecting royalty money somewhere.

Listening to the cafe commentary it became obvious that the non-Indigenous population of the town felt jilted and hurt. Local business people were worried sick. Panic had set in when the tourist trade plummeted. Tourists began cancelling their package tours to the Red Centre. Some frustrated tourists had voiced their distress, questioning whether the Australian police force had killed the local Aboriginal population in a clandestine government-mandated land theft.

Finishing his coffee Trevor walked along the mall. It seemed strange not to see his family members sitting on the grass outside the church, singing out and offering paintings for sale. He wandered through the near empty shopping centre on his way to the tavern. A sign on the locked door read 'Open At Four'. Trevor shook his head in amazement and traced his footsteps back. As he neared the shops he heard loud shouts, followed by a police siren. People rushed out of buildings to investigate, and Trevor decided to follow.

Police were arresting several civilians on the Court House lawns;

very loud civilians. Trevor noticed beer cans everywhere and realised they were drunk. He spotted Beck in the crowd and decided to walk closer. He overheard one copper joking with another, and learnt that the drinkers were redundant Centrelink employees: maybe the ennui of retrenchment had motivated them to breach the 'dry town' alcohol restrictions. Trevor stared around at the gathering crowd; no one else seemed affected by the irony. He waved at Beck, but again failed to catch her eye.

Trevor felt angry as he walked to the nearest lookout and climbed the escarpment. This hill had been a fun place he had shared with his brothers, hidden away when they needed a charge. He felt alone as he sat looking out from his vantage point. Slowly he began to hum the Song; the Song his tjamu had sung to him in Melbourne. He knew he had to get ready for tomorrow, to prepare for the role bestowed on him. He continued to sit there until dusk. Then he walked quickly along the bank of the river, towards Number Six.

The Town Camp was obviously abandoned; even the dogs were gone. New six-foot temporary cyclone fencing propped on poles and concrete post feet surrounded the perimeter, and Trevor had to break in. During the night he watched security patrol cars cruise slowly past every two hours, their spotlights invading the darkness. Trevor considered lighting a fire but was too fearful of being discovered. It was so eerie, no dogs barking, no loud music or singing, no yelling. He hardly slept.

As the dawn broke, crows shrieked at him, scampering toward his prostrate body wrapped in a blanket inside the alcove on the verandah. After his restless night Trevor enjoyed the risk of breaking out of the compound, leaving no trace as he'd done on his entry. He began to feel more reassured as he walked away from the houses, through the bush; the morning air was chilly and revived him. He heard himself humming the rhythm of the Song as he checked the landmarks to his destination. The soil began to turn redder the further he walked. He pulled his red band from his knapsack and tied it around his forehead. He felt proud, feeling so closely connected with this country. He always felt like this when he came back here. He called greetings to the kangaroos and lizards along the way, noticed the eagles soaring over him, and finches gathering in numbers. The sun was setting, and he watched as an orange and purple campfire spread across the sky. He paused when he came to the secret valley.

The distant hum of the Gate grew louder as he neared the sand hill. He pulled the tin box from his knapsack and gently placed it on the red sand. He began to sing the Song again, the words reverberating against the rocky hillside. He smiled when he saw his tjamu and the other men approaching. He noticed that his tjamu was no longer limping.

The men spoke to Trevor using gesture language. No words were uttered yet the Song grew forceful around them. Nightfall was racing in and the men gestured to Trevor to light a fire. After they left, he sat waiting, staring at the flames. He noticed that the tin box was gone.

The first pinkness touched the morning sky as eagles whistled overhead. Hundreds of finches darted around in the nearby trees. As the light increased Trevor noticed many groups of kangaroos gathered amongst the rocks that lay randomly along the length of the valley. At first he did not notice the stilling of the Song. It was the silence that made him turn, staring in disbelief.

Aboriginal people were milling everywhere, filling the valley. He recognised so many people in the crowd; all his missing family were there. A soft blue light wafted from the entrance of the Gate. Everyone was smiling in that special glow. Trevor noticed his nana in the crowd waving to him. 'Thank you Grandson,' she smiled before turning and walking away. He wanted to cry out for her but no noise erupted from his mouth.

'She not gone far,' his tjamu reassured him, suddenly by his side. Tjamu held the tin box in his hands. 'Good job you carry it back,' he said. 'Good days now,' he smiled. 'We all enjoy a bit of heaven.' Trevor smiled at the old man as they joined the crowd walking back toward the town. Everyone walking together, except the children, who skipped in the sun.

First published in *This Country Anytime Anywhere: an anthology of new Indigenous writing from the Northern Territory* (IAD Press, 2010)

Black Lives Matter

Sonya Rankine

Whiteness
White privilege
Whiteness decides if it's bad for blacks
Whiteness tells our stories
     downplays our stories
     don't know our stories
Whiteness don't know how it feels
     Becoming whitesplaining

Empathy is misguided
Empathy now used as a tool
     now becoming paternalistic
     now becoming degrading

Just listen is all we ask
Just see it is all we ask
Acknowledge is all we ask
Believe is all we ask

Know that we know what we need
As we know our truths

Blak Nation
Noah Amundson

Australia
They call it the lucky country
                    We call it home
They call themselves proud aussies
                    I call myself Arrernte
They came and stole
Attempting to seize control
Terra Nullius
A colonial proclamation
                    Millennia of Country thriving
Centuries of exploitation
Struggles of surviving
Trauma echoes
                    My grandfather
Family separation
Forced assimilation
Stolen generation
Forced by the white invasion
Referendum
Recognition
No reconciliation
                    My birth
Report
After Report
Data and statistics
Describing Blak characteristics
Recorded documentation
Tick-box consultation,
Self-serving collaboration

Apology given
    To Blak Nation
For strength and tribulation
Where's the reformation?
Racist legislation
Destroyed documentation
Where's the reparation?

    Family reconnection
    Sacred conversation
    Survives
    Reclamation
    Resistance
    Restoration
   Strong Blak Nations
   Built by Elders
   Mothers, Fathers
   Aunties, Uncles
   Sisters, Brothers

Pasts and Futures
Here and present
   Fuelled by self-determination
   Supporting next generation
   Blak Sovereign Nation

Green Thumb

Brooke Scobie

Honey suckle tongue
Snapdragon fingertips
Not green and verdant
Over-watered so drowning
They lived and died
By their father's thumb

Earth soil
Dredged into rivers
Taken with the speed of the wind
While fish float bellies up
Root systems ripped by metal beasts
And their father's thumb

Muddied waters
A torrent of too tight grips
And briny eyes
Memories of their honeysuckle tongue
Now bittered and missing
Torn out by their father's thumb

Untended twisted
Their veins barbed
Sharpened tools pricked fingers
Sucked down blood
Iron filled replacing sandy hills
Under their father's thumb.

So, roots withered
Birthed and buried
Now burnt and cracked
Ravenous thirst for long lost waterways
No longer washed away
By their father's thumb

Stood still
Pushed down pressure
Glorified and sedimentary
Dust blown skin now desert tongue
No hint of sprouted hope
Till they cut off their father's thumb.

Things Change
Lulu Houdini

She and I are at the cascade waterfalls at the end of my road. It is our second non-date. This morning I slipped it on, so carefully. Admiring how it fit. How well it hugged the swaying curves of my own personal architecture. It is hard and shiny – solid from its cast. It wasn't gifted or made for me. The words 'things change' weren't engraved on it for me. It wasn't upon me that it was measured for size, for wearability. And still my finger bridges the distance between metal and flesh flawlessly. It is heavy. I never complain under its weight. The words 'things change' wrap my fourth finger – defiance to a patriarchy, to a system that never had me in mind. Aren't we all wed to impermanence anyway? We are all changing bodies and elastic hearts.

We are in the faded eucalypt kingdom. Pools punctuate the rough stone while flowing water smooths it when it rains. She's with me. It's a date we're half in, half out of. Hesitant to call it, we continue to float in the unnamed wind and platonic warmth, slowly. We're sitting at the edge of the rockpools. We learn about each other little by little. We're talking about children; the ones we love, and the ones we are yet to love. We discuss things like timelines, fertility and ageing, the environment. River and earth hold a conversation between women that's been had forever. Unchanged. A friend told me last month about a village of women who became depressed once the washing machine arrived at their community – no longer meeting down by the riverbank to wash their families' clothing. To speak about their spouses. To air their dreams. To free their secrets imprisoned behind teeth, and custom. To bring long-ago story, forward to a river. It is important that we are here. It is important the swelling river is spoken to.

The loud tones of the water marimba beat down on rocks that were here before us and don't really notice us at all. I notice us, but also the things here that are not us. As a woman of Country seeing what most don't is sometimes an isolating experience. Until the river starts talking back.

Like a temple of understanding she always replies with something prophetic that I absorb as she speaks. I just let her words hit me. I lose the cognisance of listening. I like how all the different tattoos on the upper part of her left thigh and hip crease show their lifespan through the various shades of faded ink inside skin – how the sun has helped with that. I'm all spilling out everywhere. My beloved bikini top is too small, still, but you can't throw anything away once it's been woven. I notice how we set ourselves up against this backdrop. I come here often, she's seeing the waterfalls for the first time. I splay out and she sits with her limbs contained. She's ebb, I'm flow. We carefully select the pools, which bodies of water to place ourselves into. Which currents we can bear and which ones we can't – or don't want to. I notice the different rock friends we let touch our whole, mostly naked, bodies as we sprawl ourselves across them. Rocks never have to wait for a second date for that.

It is late summer, and our conversation has become as dense as the humid air travelling between us. Everything is moving in the space – not just the raging falls next to us and the spray it has evoked – but all the ripe and brimming possibilities that exist for us. All the things we call into our lives. Bringing her here, to my favourite patch of Kabi Kabi Country, feels like introducing her to my parents.

Sweaty, I enter the water with the same urgency of everything in this landscape demanding to be seen. I jump in, feet first into my favourite of the deep pools. I enter the water and I exit the world of land; the certainties of ground are left behind. My hands in the air, I feel myself glide. It happens quickly but I feel it like slow motion. Each of our skins meet slowly – the waters and mine. Fingertips last. Disappearing is my latest pastime as a young and single woman.

I revel in how good it feels to be washed. How effective this cold freshwater is at erasing my plans and thoughts. How good it feels underwater with no wind. When my toes touch the ground of reeds and mud, I kick off, ready for my certain and promised rebirth. My ring exits my finger. A fluid motion, off and into fluid. I resurface with a lightness not knowing what's gone. It's being hurried down the rapids, onto a greater body also made of water. Or perhaps it's sinking softly to the bottom of this pool, just happy to be settling. I was happy, to be settling.

The sun rewarms my bones and I wait for a visit from the sky dancers, the dragonflies. I look over at her; she's all brown skin and form. All rigid, rising muscles, with a softness incorporating everything. She's like curved water, a synonym for dense softness. She breathes so slowly, like a soft machine. I look down to my palms, unaware of what's left me. Until I am. Somehow, the familiar landscape of my hand is no longer so familiar. With a stinging pang all over I notice that my ring is gone. A light, dull ache after impact, arrives to my brow.

I don't say anything at first. I let it hit then disperse. It doesn't hurt, it never hurt. I continue to let our conversation, her words, be the background lighting as I ponder. I let her voice float across my ears and body. I meet her eyes – to let her know I'm here. But I'm not really here. A memory of this morning glides over my mind and I involuntarily laugh at this image of myself putting my ring on for a non-date at the waterfall at the end of my road. Like I wanted or needed in some way to detox that heavy metal – that 200 grams of pure 925 silver. Like a baby tooth I needed to lose, or the lesson you don't want.

When I am done with acknowledging my loss alone, I let her know what happened. I tell her how I've been working on stopping the habit of saying, 'It's fine.' I accept the irony of my 'things change' ring being slipped off my finger and on to exist somewhere else. To change something else. I hope the fish are happy down there, pondering their literal message of detachment sent from sky Country – from me.

She is attentive – offers me fruit as salve. My tongue wasn't bitter but I am grateful for all the sweetness. Revelations in new lightness. I think back to last month when I asked the ultramarine Pacific Ocean – 'Everything changes, so why can't I?' A punctuated night sky reminds me – everything in nature changes, so why wouldn't you? Everything recedes and decays, or both. We all lose. We learn another way.

She came and went with the summer – arriving and departing on perfect time. The feeling of a flowing river under our house compels us to emerge anew after loss, fantastically raw and beautiful, hope in our step. I return to the river's pebbled shores and beating chorus. I think about that symbol. Like all the things that changed against a willingness to let them – we remain changelings. We are not the possessions in our lives, like furnishings to our personhood. We are what we become as a result of having and losing them. We are like that solid piece of silver – marked by things that change.

Disparaging

Sheena Hayes

I met you unexpectedly
I had no intention of dating
You weren't my type of guy
I thought I'd give you a chance

As time passed
I got to know you
And slowly,
I grew
To like you

The wall I had built to keep everyone away from me
Was crumbling away
I told you about
The demons that pervaded my dreams
And for awhile
You were my rescuer
Who slayed those monsters

I would get lost in our conversations and time would fly so quickly
Our time together
Was blissful

You brought me
The much-needed peace
That I had been yearning for so long

And then that
Moment had arrived
You said to me
'I sense you want
Something more serious
To happen between us'

I did my job well
I led you to
Assume this idea
I had already decided that
There was no place for you
In my life

I was horrible
I had revealed so much
That I felt the need to betray

I was gonna sabotage
Whatever our vibes we had felt
I didn't play hard to get
I had used you to distract me

The truth is
I already cared for someone else
You seemed to ease my loneliness
But only for awhile

Every time we kissed
Your kisses were bitter
Like the wine you sipped
There was always him
In the back of my mind
Which is why I always pulled away from you

But who knew
I would get hurt like this
I played with fire
And I got burned

But don't worry about me
I'm gonna be fine
The wall you broke down
I have been slowly piecing together the bricks to rebuild a better wall

I can't bear to look at you
My adoration for you
Has turned into the black beast
I don't want to see you anymore
From this moment onwards
It was as if you never existed
We had never crossed paths
I would prefer it this way
Goodbye

You say Aborigine, I say Blak

Dylan 'Muldari Kor:ni' Peisley

I'm sick

I'm sick of hearing about another death
Untrained men stealing Uncle's last breath
I'm sick of the lack of change
Almost five hundred deaths, isn't it strange

I'm sick and I'm tired

I'm tired of forever looking over my shoulder
Wondering if I'll see my little sister grow older
I'm tired of those blaring sirens that have me flinching
Scared that now is the time for my lynching

I'm tired and I'm hurt

I'm hurt that I'm judged by the colour of my skin
Assimilated into a colony I don't belong in
I'm hurt that my culture has been erased
Leaving nothing but racism and bad taste

I'm hurt and I'm bitter

I'm bitter that I'm made to feel bad that I'm Blak
Their aggressive slurs are like knives to my back
I'm bitter that I'll die ten years sooner
Because those white settlers had a sick sense of humour

I'm bitter and I'm mad

I'm mad every time some white fulla claims
'I know what's best, no need for games'
I'm mad that they caused this terror and set our land aflame
And then turn to us fullas like we're to blame

I'm mad and I'm sad

I'm sad that the home to our dreaming that we share
Has become host to this bloody nightmare
I'm sad that I'm 17 times more likely to be in jail
Because I'm living while being a strong black male

I'm sad and I'm angry

I'm angry that this colony is keeping me down
Just because the colour of my skin is fucking brown
I'm angry that I'm always followed around the shops
Like damn man, when will it stop

I'm angry and I'm proud

I'm proud to be Aboriginal
The first culture, the original
I'm proud of my ancestors
And all my brothers and sisters

I'm proud to be Blak
A defender of country, protector of sea
A Blak future, just my mob and me

My Body Remembers

Taryn Poole

My body, doesn't keep time
it keeps memories, though
are they my father's, or are they mine?
they are the only ones I know
I am one half of him
but I am ALL that blak sin
the weight of past generations, embossed on my skin
the wait of generations, baying to begin

my body, doesn't keep time
it keeps a score though
through our DNA, they've bided time
our ancestors, and all they know
all those paths they show
the stars they make glow
the stories wanting to be known
called up from the grit of this earth, we call home

my body, doesn't keep time
it knows this place though
it knows its own kind
they are my father's ilk, they are all mine
I hear them cry when I cry
I can feel how they died
I can feel them, bound to this place
echoing in our songs, never to be erased

my body, doesn't keep time
but it knows what was lost here
it remembers generations of love
it remembers generations of fear
it echoes across divides
it calls us home, by our names
the result of a living, breathing culture
it reminds me that you and I, are not the same

my body, doesn't keep time
but it will never forget
it won't let go
it knows no regret
it is love bleeding through pain
hope overpowering the shame
the denial of your names

my body doesn't keep time
but regardless of you, it holds this space
an outline of our family
it holds every trace
and our connection to this time
catching on the wind as it whines
harkens back to our place
with the seasons that tide

my body won't keep time
and it won't keep pace
when I am gone
my connection keeps me to this place
I will return to the sacred dirt
given back to this earth
with my ancestors, our ghosts
with generations of love and of hope
I will always be home.

Dedicated to our sister Kez and the loving memory we hold

Sail

Edoardo Crismani

Don't put upon my reason
Don't put upon my hope
For the fires of jealousy
Burn a penance with a rope

And underneath the bridge of night
That beast can hold you tight
For who knows the boat's safety
Until it is ashore

Those that never venture out
Only know the shore
But I taste the pain
Blood in vain

Whipped across my back
And until the last adventure
I sail
For more

The Old People
Ben Armstrong

Bururrgan and Dirragarra were finishing up breakfast in their camp, before making the last leg of their journey to meet with the person who may be able to help them with the job they have taken on. It's a suspicious request to help a company called Right Lands that on the surface sounds legitimate, but under the surface doesn't seem to respect or acknowledge sovereignty and Ancestors. That is why this trip is so important.

Bururrgan, or Buru to Dirragarra, is Straw-necked Ibis-folk, which is quite rare to see. He has rather typical black and white plumage, and is unassuming in his presence and demeanour. His long white neck is adorned with a small pearlescent butterfly-designed bowtie and he wears a tweed vest, with a handkerchief in his chest pocket that matches his beautiful neck adornment. Due to the destruction of their ancestral homes, the Straw-necked Ibis-folk were displaced and had to move into the major towns. The towns were and continue to be unfamiliar places for them. They had trouble finding work because they never needed jobs before. So most of them began searching for whatever food they could find to feed their families. They would search in the fields, streets and even sometimes the rubbish tip, which resulted in them being labelled 'Bin Chickens'. This is why Bururrgan is meticulous with his appearance and pays particular attention to ensuring his feathers are smooth and pin free, to shake free of the negative imagery of his folk that unfairly gets bandied around.

Dirragarra, or Dirra to Bururrgan, is Wambad-folk, short and stocky, hairy and gruff, strong as the earth and yet as kind as a cool breeze during wet season. However, his motto is most definitely 'muck around and find out'. He often carries a large backpack almost overflowing with food, and wears nothing more than modest covering and a few belts to hang essentials from. Dirragarra is incredibly strong and has a set of powerful claws that come in handy in a number of ways, one of which is filling in his little trench-like hole that he sleeps in. Dirragarra's mob are more common than Bururrgan's and can be found across the eastern lands. There are a few different tribes of Wambad-folk, some shorter with hairier noses, others large and built like walking boulders. All of them live in underground dwellings commonly referred to as 'The Burrow', hinting that even though they are different mobs they share common Ancestors.

Bururrgan and Dirragarra first met half a dozen seasons ago, near Dirragarra's home. Dirragarra was taking a break from digging extension tunnels for his mob, sipping on myrtle tea and eating snow-grass cookies when he heard a call for help. He ran in the direction of the alarm and found Bururrgan at the base of a large gum pleading with a Yugay assailant. The stories say that once upon a time they were proud Dingo-folk but they made a deal with an evil spirit and now they are cursed as Yugay, to roam the lands preying on anyone and anything in their path. Dirragarra rushed in to tackle the Yugay without concern for himself but just as he closed in, the Yugay bit down on Bururrgan! Or so the Yugay and Dirragarra believed. Bururrgan has spent many years honing his skills and developing his unassuming presence to deceive and trick even the most alert folk. The Yugay bit down on nothing more than an illusion of Bururrgan, and straight onto a thistle bush, filling its mouth with burning thistle spines. It yelped furiously, turned to see Dirragarra barrelling in, and ran, tail between its legs. Dirragarra looked up at Bururrgan sitting in a nearby tree branch preening a wing feather and let out a booming laugh. Bururrgan shortly joined in, and since then they have been inseparable.

They had camped between the long grass and the water's edge of a nearby river, in a flat section of dirt and roots just below the upper grass line, down a sloping section of the riverbank. The river hadn't been at full flow for a few years now, and while this offered a well-protected area to rest, it made Bururrgan wonder what had happened to the water as he looked across the top of it, mesmerised at the small ripples forming from water skimmers and fish feeding on insects. It was as serene a spot as they could have wished for the night – a good place to rest after a long day's walk. There were large gums and acacias on either side of the riverbank. Various species of callistemons in full bloom line the edge of the riverbanks, looking like drips of ochre from the Great Old Ones that created the canvas that we walk upon today. It was a humbling reminder to Bururrgan, especially as this was not his country.

'Argh, we didn't bring enough food Buru,' grumbles Dirragarra, as he tightens the string on the top of his very full backpack.

'We'll find some fruits on the way Dirra,' comforts Bururrgan as he continues to be lost in the view. He sees a palm tree on the other bank of the river and for a moment his mind drifts away to more peaceful nights, sleeping in the great trees of his homeland with flock, with family, with Ancestors.

His contemplation breaks when Dirragarra throws a swag at him. 'You gonna help or wha bra?' the Wambad-folk exclaims.

Bururrgan smiles, collects the swag, walks past Dirragarra, and as he does so he deftly tucks the remainder of his morning's damper into one of the Dirragarra's belts unnoticed. Bururrgan is after all a put-pocket, a retired thief now bringing joy to people through the act of surprise giving without expecting recompense.

'Let's get a move on Dirra, there is still quite a way to go and I would like to get there before the Bat-folk awake ... or worse,' Bururrgan suggests.

Dirragarra nods in agreement then says, 'And we gotta find some more food as well aye, keep up our strength.' And he flexes in a power pose for dramatic exclamation.

It is never a dull day with this one, Bururrgan thinks, as he smiles and pats Dirragarra on the back. 'Let's be off then.'

Most of the day passes, with a few stops here and there to collect lilli pillis and passionfruit, before the duo arrive at a marking. This marking identifies the end of the country they are on and the beginning of the country they may be about to walk upon. It is a unique set of old paperbark gums that lean towards each other, growing together as if they are embracing one another. A depiction of two women can be seen where the paperbark is shedding from the trees, clear as the sun on a blue-sky day. They are Corinna-folk, old people, in the embrace. As soon as Bururrgan and Dirragarra see this they feel warmth and kindness wash over them, but also a warning.

'Gorn then,' Dirragarra states.

Bururrgan walks up to this sacred place. He takes out two carved wooden figures, one of an Ibis-folk and another a Wambad-folk, and he places them in front of the trees. 'I acknowledge the Old People of this sacred body that we wish to walk upon. We bring no harm, we will walk with respect and we will leave when requested. We ask for entrance to walk on Corinna Country and offer these gifts as a token of our respect for the Sovereign Corinna People, the Ancestors and Elders, the Young Ones and Bubs.'

Bururrgan turns around and walks back to Dirragarra, who nods at him. They sit, and wait. All around them the air is filled with the buzzing of cicadas and bees. The wind gently flows through the tree branches and leaves, blessing them with some cool respite. Life is all around them, and it is Dirragarra this time who is lost in contemplation.

He looks up into the trees and says, 'Ya know Buru, I miss the tunnels and grass of 'ome but true god, if this isn't one of the most magical places I ever have bin!'

Bururrgan smiles. His long-time friend and adventuring companion does not often get lost in the places around him, preferring more to get lost in food or trouble, so he lets this moment linger as the sun starts to lower below the top of the trees, threatening to set soon.

'Ah!' Bururrgan exclaims and he stands up.

'Ere what is it bruz?' Dirragarra says as he jumps up at the ready.

'You don't smell that Dirra? We've been welcomed, initially at least, we must walk quickly and honour my words, friend. This way,' Bururrgan says, as he picks up his things and starts walking off between the great paperbark trees.

Dirragarra takes a long, deep breath in through his nose, puffing out his barrel-like chest, and picks up the softest scent of burning eucalyptus leaves. With a great breath out, he too grabs his overflowing backpack, and walks off after Bururrgan, nodding respectfully at the Ancestors as he passes them.

After a short walk, they arrive at a single storey house. The sun is now lower in the sky, barely skimming the tops of the blooming acacias, like the sun setting over great golden sand dunes. The house is constructed with old wooden slats, some with visible holes where the knots in the wood have fallen out, and a dark grey slate roof. There is smoke rising from the roof, assumingly from a chimney on the opposite side. There is a wooden balcony that encircles the house, making it seem larger and offering some much-needed shade on hot days. Warm light streams out of the window on the right side of the front door, where the curtains are still half drawn to the side. A lantern is fixed to the front balcony post, offering a small welcoming glow, and more than a few fluttering insects are bathing in and out of its light. Bururrgan's and Dirragarra's eyes are quickly drawn to the old lady rocking back and forth in a rocking chair on the balcony, to the left of the front door. The chair creaks with each rock, back and forth and back again, and the old lady draws in on the loosie in her mouth, as if the glow of that smoke is in tune with the creaks. Next to her is a small table with a cast-iron teapot and three earthy-looking ceramic cups with steam rising from them. The adventuring couple pause, and wait for the lady to welcome them into her space. Even though they were welcomed to walk here, there are protocols to follow and she is clearly an Elder; her space and her place are sacred, and she is never alone.

'Ere now you two, come and sit, you've travelled far and best know I'm not for making you bubs stand out there all night ay,' the old lady says.

'Thank you Aunt … ah … I'm sorry, we were never told who we were to meet,' Bururrgan replies.

She looks up and smiles, the light from the balcony lantern and her glowing loosie smoke illuminates her face in an otherworldly glow. 'I'm Nan Rose and you can call me Nan Rose,' she clarifies.

An old Corinna-folk Elder, she is not tall, about the same height as Dirragarra. Her fur is short and greying but her most striking feature is the tattoo of a rose that adorns her face. The rose petals are bright red, without any dullness in colour from age. It's either a new tattoo or exceptional quality. The flower starts up on her forehead, and then the stem of the rose curls down, along her face and onto her chin. She has a lone tooth that sticks out from her lip, and it joins the tattoo perfectly so that it represents a thorn on the rose stem. From that tooth there is a drip of blood tattooed to look like someone has pricked their hand on it. As Dirragarra sits down on the balcony floor he swears he sees that drip of blood move, as if it was animated. When he looks up at Nan Rose she smiles back at him.

'Welcome to my home. Would like some myrtle tea and mealworm biscuits?' Nan Rose offers, as she starts to hand them cups of pre-poured tea, wholly expecting them to accept the invitation.

'Thank you, Nan Rose,' both Dirragarra and Bururrgan say in sync, and they take the tea and a biscuit, even though they don't normally eat mealworms, as it's protocol to accept.

'Well, who are ya? Who sent ya? And why are ya here?' Nan Rose asks, before taking a long sip of her warm tea.

Bururrgan responds first, 'My name is Bururrgan, I'm from Ibis Country, from the flock of the Straw-Necked.'

'And I'm Dirragarra. I was born and raised on Wambad Country, them Tunnel Mob,' Dirragarra says, as some crumbs roll down his front.

'We were hired to help a company but it didn't feel right, so we asked a young fulla in town who we knew was from around these ways, and he said we should come here and speak with the Elder,' adds Bururrgan.

Nan Rose stops rocking her chair and leans forward, 'Ahhh nephew has done well, cos you don't wanna be helping those corporate dogs that work for Giggy Mineheart.'

Giggy Mineheart. That's a name they have heard before, but it was never mentioned in the request for help from Right Lands. Mineheart is as evil as they come, profiting off stolen land, placing profits over everything else, including the lives of people. They knew there was something suspicious about this job and Nan Rose just confirmed it.

Nan Rose continues with a growl to her voice, 'They are up on the hill carving into us! Like a razor on our bare skin. This gammin young one thought they would make a big name for themselves ay, a self-professed "lore-man", barely got hairs. He sold away the rights to that place like he owned it, and then left. Probably grovelling for scraps at Mineheart's feet. Now we have a problem cos the Ancestors are angry and they are taking them workers up there, rightfully so too …' Nan Rose pauses, and takes a long draw on the loosely packed smoke dangling from the left side of her mouth to calm herself a little. She continues, 'But it means more people have come ya see, with weapons to protect them workers and now we got a fight on our hands.'

Bururrgan and Dirragarra look at each other knowingly, they knew this type of story was becoming more common. They have lived it, they have seen the impact and displacement and they have heard the yarns at every stop of their journey. Whether it's the trees being felled at Bururrgan's ancestral home, or excavation on Dirragarra's and other Wambad-folk's lands, the impact to all Mob was brushed over as a necessary casualty of 'advancement'. It felt like death by a thousand cuts.

'How can we help youse Nan Rose?' Dirragarra asks, sits up with the anger of his people's history and the realisation that this is happening to Mob on many lands – it floods his emotions and has become worn on his face.

Nan Rose stares at them for what feels to Bururrgan and Dirragarra like an eternity, like every moment of their life was being assessed. After a minute or two, Nan Rose smiles, moving the thorn-like tooth along the tattoo stem causing a new drop of magical tattoo blood to flow down her chin.

'Destroy this mine, this injustice, this wound upon our bodies.

Seal it up so that we may start to heal bubs. Get them folk working there to leave, if you can. They are disrespecting us and I want no more bloodshed on our land. You let them know that's the only way those folks stop going home in boxes if that's what it takes for them to understand.'

Bururrgan and Dirragarra stand, with strength in their legs and staunchness in their hearts. They say in unison, as if driven by some greater power, 'We'll help your Mob, Nan Rose.'

Nan Rose smiles and nods, 'For the Old People!'

Queen Victoria's throne no more
Tabitha Lean

I stand at the base of her granite throne
wondering at her voluminous curves
her steely gaze
regal robes
I've always lingered here, for too long
resting my feet on Kaurna soil
as the cars zoom by
the traffic lights glow
pedestrians patter
commuters flow

Every time I stand here the world folds in.
pavers turn on their sides and slide into the ground
the streetlights disappear
bitumen crumbles
as the trees rise higher into the sky
the monotonous drone of the traffic sighs
cement gives way to dirt
grass returns to soil

I feel myself shrink
my newly small palm
enveloped in another's clasp
I glance up and peer through squinted eyes
to see my mother,
who is earthbound
after 45 years of resting
    in the dreaming.
as the sun glows behind her

she has an ethereal quality
befitting an angel

She smiles a smile I don't remember
through eyes I can't recall
a voice that is vaguely familiar
Come child she beckons
pulling me gently away
my small feet trail two steps behind her neck twisted in rear view
my eyes still fixed on Victoria
mother glides across the square
tightrope walking on gossamer
strings of spider webs

As we move the terrain alters
shape shifting before me
grey gives way to brown, green
buildings fall and shrubbery rises
dust swirls
I feel the heartbeat of the land
quake through my body

Tarntanyangga is reborn
we stand at the base of another world
'a kingdom, my daughter
a kingdom rose that day
five years before you took breath
not one she rules,'
mother motioned her chin towards Victoria

but this one
my mother's cornflower blue eyes rose to the sky
mine followed hers up the steel pole
to the billowing flag dancing gleefully in the wind
'A kingdom of red, black and yellow
the colours of our rule, my daughter
kings and queens of this land
caretakers
rightful owners'

'Oh she knows not what governance is
taking what is not hers
they have some cheek standing her here
on this land, in this place
Stand at the feet of this throne my girl
worship this world
for this is our place
our space
forever more'

'When civilisations crumble
and the world collapses
our spirits will remain
because the gentle giant rests
in the crust of this earth.
He lives and breathes in you, my girl
but for now
you take one step each day
you listen to the whisper

of the wind
for I will send you missives
in the rustle of the leaves
and we'll meet again in this place
dear girl,
beneath the flag that rose that day.'

And as a gust of wind swept past my ankles
and lifted into the sky unfurling the flag
billowing its colours against the clouds
I rose to stand alone
in the square of colonial creation
with Victoria at one end
and the flag of my people at the other –
bookended by both colonialism and creation
but before I could draw breath
I felt the land sigh
the cars started driving
the birds flying and
commuters commuting –
the square came back to life
and just like that
I put one foot in front of the other
and listened for the rustle of the leaves.

Campfire
Kathryn Gledhill-Tucker

When we build a campfire, we send a beacon. A bright burning ember unravels, consuming bark and oxygen until it burns bright enough to be seen from the sky. We gather, tell stories, bathe in its smoke; keep ourselves, and culture, alive. When we are feeling homesick or inexplicably unwell we say 'Go back to the campfire,' and know we will find the comfort of spirit in the smoke.

The woman sitting across from me on this train has one of those pet carriers with a plastic bubble, designed for the animal to see out into the world while still being protected. The bag itself is floral and sturdy, and she is clutching the strap with one hand while lightly tapping the lid with the other. 'We're heading to the farmers market, and then I think we should grab a coffee somewhere,' she speaks into the bag. She then gives a detailed description of the scenery outside, as the bag is positioned too low to have a view of the window. Small houses with tin roofs, blue skies pocketed with clouds, a train running in the opposite direction.

'Why don't you do that for me, bub?' I hear from the algo device strapped to my chest. Cheeky.

Most algos are the size of a small dog. Spherical and smooth, kind of like a hairless Furby. Small enough to squeeze into a handbag, or a small chest harness like the one I have fashioned for my algo, who we affectionately call Aunty.

The floral pet carrier has caught the eye of another passenger, who is far less impressed. 'Ridiculous,' he says. Next to him, his wife softly tries to coax him not to be rude to strangers. He leans over across the aisle, 'It's not real, you know?'

I smile sympathetically to the woman, as she shuffles the carrier to the other side of her seat. 'It looks like a pretty comfortable home,' I remark. The man makes more disparaging comments to no one in particular, but loud enough for our section of the train to get an earful of ranting. He says loudly, 'She's treating it like a child!'

His wife gets out of her seat to alight the train, and tells him again to stop bothering the woman. Unfortunately, this is my stop, too. I hold my harness a little more closely as we step onto the platform. Behind us, a train guard picks up the algo the man has left on his seat, and hands it back to him, 'You don't want to leave this behind, Sir.' I suspect he probably does.

Since the *Algorithmic Transparency Act* was passed, machines with a microprocessor capable of capturing, storing, or analysing data, or generating new inferences based on data, must have a physical presence that is not obscured from view of the analysed subject. On some level of course we knew we were surrounded by invisible algorithms, watching our behaviour and learning our personalities, to feed us more relevant information or search engine results or advertisements. But now that they take a physical form – now that we carry these algorithms around in our bags, talk to them, care for them – their presence is unmissable. Burdensome, to some, but many of us have grown quite fond of the things. My algo holds as much information about my person as can be reduced to bits and bytes. It knows me better than anybody.

I take mostly back routes from the train station to my apartment. Lush streets lined with jacaranda trees and fewer surveillance cameras, except at one unavoidable intersection. Standing at the pedestrian crossing, I tap the button. I realise this probably does nothing substantial, but does make me feel like I have some agency despite the traffic light algorithm.

I bury my hands into my armpits while I wait for the light to turn green. 'Hey there, cold hands. Where are you headed?'

I ignore the computer-generated voice coming from the traffic light and wait for the light to turn green.

'It's a bit of a wait. Peak hour here.' The traffic light fetches data from the machine on the opposite side of the road to confirm its estimates. 'Pete, how much longer?' Longer than usual because a few impatient drivers have paid the extra subscription fee for shorter red lights on their commute.

The traffic light tries to engage me again. 'Can I connect to your algo? I could try and make this light go faster for you.'

I decline. I'm in no hurry, and I have a habit of opting out whenever I get the chance. While I'm waiting, I catch the traffic light making an attempt at profiling. When I refuse to tell it my date of birth, allegedly so the Department of Infrastructure can wish me a happy birthday, the machine asks prompts to narrow my demographic; old Simpsons references, a few 90s albums, in which federal election I was first eligible to vote. AI machines are not allowed to connect to people's algos without explicit consent, but there is a grey area around conversationally derived metadata. People are more likely to give up sensitive information if they think they are engaging in a friendly, non-threatening chat, but not everybody agrees as to whether this kind of data collection is manipulative or coercive. The machine struggles to place my ethnicity and runs through a list of European and Middle Eastern countries. 'I'm from here,' I say sharply.

Not satisfied with that categorisation, the traffic light asks the question I find most loathsome in the world: 'No, where are you *really* from?'

'Nyorn,' Aunty clicks her tongue in disappointment. I consider jaywalking to escape the electro-small talk, but spot public transport guards patrolling the train station on the next street over. Plus, this traffic light has several sensing cameras circled around the top of its post, worn like a heavy bracelet.

The Act was designed in response to the kind of invisible or obfuscated algorithms popularised by 'smart' cities. Public spaces had become filled with computers designed to enhance the function of a city, but this created new vulnerabilities and concerns. As these cities became more prolific, there was growing public sentiment that being constantly tracked was highly invasive and created a culture of normalised surveillance. People wanted to know what data was being captured, where it was stored, and who had access.

Overnight, there was a massive proliferation of new structures set up around the city. Streets were suddenly cluttered with conspicuous cameras and recording devices at every corner. Buildings were haphazardly adorned with gaudy electronics nestled into cornices. These devices had, of course, always been there with an invisible footprint. At first, the mess of new machines were considered an eyesore but their presence quickly became commonplace, much like charging stations or playground swings. Machines were smothered with graffiti as activists made the most of these new canvases. 'Smart Asinine City.' 'Evict Big Brother.'

Technology vendors, initially aggrieved by the idea of opening the black box of marketing algorithms and the burden of compliance, found people wanted to touch, play, and interact with these new additions to the city. Experts in human-centred design relished the opportunity to explore this new field of machine interaction and anthropomorphism. CCTV cameras were fixed with oversized, blinking eyes as they surveyed the populace. Smart water fountains greeted you with huggable arms as you filled up your recycled flask, which children loved. Businesses discovered that machines augmented with conversational algorithms had higher rates of interaction and attention duration, and people were generally more sympathetic towards computers with a personality. Quiet spaces were increasingly impossible to find as the city filled with the incessant chatter of data-driven conversation.

This is why today, in the name of algorithmic transparency, I am getting harassed by a traffic light.

Before the transport guards make their way to my corner of the street, the light turns green, and I step closer to home. Even though I opt to stay disconnected from public machines, I suspect my algo is responsible for the good fortune. Thanks, Aunty.

Erin's and my front door wears a faint scar from the smart lock we removed a few months earlier and replaced with an old brass lock. This now discarded smart lock had a plaid blue suit and tie, and would chatter to every passer-by in an Irish accent at inconvenient times. Most conversations were innocuous, but one evening, with our ears pressed to the door, we heard one side of a concerning conversation that sounded conspiratorial. Then, my housemate and I learned how much information was being sent from our front door to some data warehouse in the United States, and the smart lock had to go. Removal was logistically challenging, and no locksmith was prepared to do the job for fear of breaching algorithm rights. In the end, we took a drill to it and sent the machine to a recycler.

'Welcome back,' my housemate Erin greets us from their room with a well-rested voice. 'Hi Aunty!' Erin's friendliness is a welcoming change to the AI mess outside.

After the smart lock incident, the apartment only has enough

Internet-of-Things devices to not relinquish the quality of life afforded by connected technology. No home assistants, no smart fridge. We tried installing a few self-hosted smart lights but couldn't overcome the personality conflicts between the devices. Kitchen bulbs wanted bright, cool lights for seeing clearly and living room lights favoured warmer tones. We brought in a technology mediator to audit our electronics installation, but the fundamental incompatibility between models was irreconcilable. After a month of bickering that manifested one evening as rapid brightening and dimming between rooms, the kitchen blew a fuse and went permanently dark.

'My algo and I are so in sync right now,' Erin tells me. From the front door of the apartment, I can see through to the lavender glow of Erin's bedroom where they have been studying at a small melamine desk. Their algo is propped up on an elaborate shrine, surrounded by a dozen pink and white crystals, a collection of zines exploring the nature of human–algo relationships, and an inoperative Tamagotchi. Erin leans back in their chair to catch my eye through the bedroom doorway. 'A tarot reader on TikTok told me this morning that I was about to have a tower moment.' I don't know what this means, but they say the word 'tower' with a flash of intensity, and apologise in advance for any chaotic behaviour over the next couple of days.

We discuss dinner plans and Erin suggests a recipe their algo told them about that involves whipping tofu. 'I've never tried doing that but I trust Al's recommendation,' Erin said.

After dinner, Aunty and I settle into a download ritual. All lights are out and the windows are open to let in the fresh air perfumed by eucalyptus swaying outside my room. Next to my computer monitor, I light a small candle with a wooden wick that crackles as it burns. I unbuckle my algo harness and remove Aunty from their seat. Walking around all day, we've gathered plenty of new data to add to the collection.

We plug into the Campfire, a distributed network of mob and our algos (the ones that sprung up about the same time as the talking traffic lights). All social media platforms come with mandatory algos, so everybody has one. It's damn near impossible to avoid social media without also giving up access to community, family, and the space we use for organising. It isn't ideal, but we make it work for us, and we are slowly learning how to communicate with better encryption.

The new Indigenous Data Sovereignty legislation has given us power to control how our algo data is stored and shared. We have been able to partition off the bits of the algo that communicate with third-party platforms, leaving a large portion of the machine free for our own use. With the algos connected together, we have created our own network of supercomputers capable of performing calculations much more advanced than the personal computers in our bedrooms. I set Aunty on top of a wireless charging pad next to my keyboard, which glows with the same orange warmth as the candle flame.

In the voice chat, Cuz is working on a new algorithm to test soil composition on his Country. He suspects a nearby gas project is illegally dumping waste into their local water supply. 'I can prove it, too.' Cuz uploads a new set of collected data to the Campfire and everybody online takes a look. A few other mob have similar datasets from their own Country that can be used for comparison. We throw around some ideas for measuring changes over time and consider incorporating satellite telemetry from local climate researchers. By the end of the evening, we have generated new charts and graphs that elicited a few 'oohs' and 'ahhs' as we peer further into the data and suggest changes.

The improvements made to Cuz's algorithm mean it is now sufficiently advanced to require its own physical holding, so we get started on a 3D model. The design starts off looking like a crude assembly of geometric objects, then somebody says it could resemble a creature that lives underground since it is working so closely with soil. 'Maybe a burrowing frog?' I suggest. The soft legs are a challenge to mock up but the end result is impressive. A beautiful creature that will be cared for as much as it cares for us.

Before powering down, Aunty uses our agreed phrase to let me know it's time to turn in: 'Two teabags. Thanks, bub.'

The Macadamia Tree
Alexis West

the Macadamia tree
    Bopple tree

that's what me and my adopted brothers called it when we were kids
I have no idea why we called them that Bopples

my first favourite macadamia tree
    grew in my adopted great grandmother's backyard

Great Grandma Morton
    shrivelled up
    tiny old white lady
lived alone in a house built by her late husband
                in the 1800s
the house was dark
full of ancient
    musty stuff
    brass crocodiles and poison
    we weren't allowed to touch

'go outside and play!'
YES! The backyard
THE JUNGLE!
    where oxygen, food and fairies lived
where my macadamia tree grew

turns out
Bopple is a black fulla word
Macadamias are native
site specific South East Queensland & Northern New South Wales
    neighbouring countries
rainforest   hinterlands   my ancestors' country
Wakka Wakka   my Country
my trees   my Bopples

intuitively us kids called them by their first name
children, old people
    open souls can hear the whisper of trees
    angels   ancestors
listening to the rememberings of the forgotten

shown how to place
    chocolate brown sphere
    into a divot on a hard bit of surface
get a hammer
    or a solid rock
    hit them precisely on the spot where the stem once grew

bang it over
    over and over
    gently but with force   til you cracked them open

BANG BANG CRACK
BANG BANG CRACK

if you don't hit 'em right   obliterated
gently,   but with force

brothers losing patience   interest
they'd run off
          playing jungle war games
pelting missile macadamias at each other
          or me
                    mostly me
I'd hide under the shelter of my Bopple tree

this special tree
displaced and replanted   Bankstown   Darug Country

like me
          displaced   replanted   adopted into a new family
in a place I didn't belong   growing

I'd hold the smooth-textured unopened Bopple
almost same colour as my skin
ohhh I would pig out
          cos I'm greedy like that
BANG BANG CRACK
I'd feel guilty for being such a greedy guts so I toil
BANG BANG CRACK
open morsels to share with my brothers
                              Mum   Dad   Grandma
opened and unopened nuts
stuffing my pockets full

Now   Great Grandma Morton's Daughter
       Grandma Hazel Gosson
       oooh she was a hard nut
I don't think she knew what to make of me
         my brown brother Andy
growing up white
    in racist Australia   early 1900s
Great War, Depression   Second World War
losing loved ones   uncles brothers friends
dying
    coming back from wars
       broken maimed traumatised
fighting for stolen land
living on stolen land
forgetting on stolen land

her son and his wife couldn't have children.
so they adopt a nice little white boy
then two brown babies
    my adopted family

Grandma Hazel's house in Revesby had three small bedrooms
a big grassy backyard
agapanthus   an outdoor dunny and hills hoist.
Mum and Dad slept in a bed
us kids slept on these uncomfortable outdoor banana lounge thingos
Granma, rightfully, in her lovely boudoir
          NO KIDS ALLOWED

Grandma would set the table nice
cooking the most wholesome feeds
one day it was only Grandma and I
        in the kitchen
I pulled her skirt to get her attention
        offered her a tasty from my pocket
she accepted it with grace
despite being such a hard nut

Days would blur over the seasons
so many visits   holidays and all the midday movies
my brothers   bored and rowdy   would go outside to play
Me   you'd have to drag me away from the television
I'd sit with a cushion cuddled into my chest
Grandma let me snuggle into her legs
my eyes wide   sucking my thumb
all the classics
gently but with force

this one time   Grandma
fed up with them boys teasing
tickling and bullying me
said it was okay for me to sleep in her bed
in her room
the mattress was soft, sheets clean and cosy
        smelled of her puff powder
no poxy banana lounge for me!
she'd complain the next morning at breakfast
that I'd kicked her   black and blue

in the middle of the night   almost out of bed
but from that point on every time we stayed with her
I got to sleep in her big bed.

I'm not saying I was her favourite
but she was mine

like macadamias
I had to patiently wait
to crack open my favourite people
gorgeous leaves and foliage   pretty   delicate flowers
the scent

they'd grow into these green clusters
ripening   forming an outer husk
waiting
patiently waiting
and then   they drop to the ground
beneath their husk   what looks like big chocolate Maltesers
they'll shatter your teeth if you try and eat 'em like that!
creamy   dreamy   kinda sweet savoury rich
their taste lingers
salty   spicy   smoky crunchy
but not too crunchy   chewy
transformative, sweet toffee'd coffee'd honeyed chocolate-covered
its oil seeps into our lives
for cooking hair conditioner body butter nutty butter
hardest nut in the world to crack
but so worth it

Rest in peace Grandma ...
I'd sit there for hours minutes decades
      days   centuries seconds years
remembering
the lost   found
the forgotten
the stolen
in that backyard
that jungle
under my Bopple tree

That Branch. It Hums

Karen Wyld

In a dry riverbed, over that way
two trees grow: an oak and bloodwood
awkwardly embracing. Convoluted
there, in that usually dry riverbed.

Green grass grows on one bank.
On the other, red dirt reaches beyond time.
A shimmer hovers above those trees
concealing, yet also illuminating.

Look. One of the interwoven branches,
that one, is snaking towards the roots.
Poor fella, looks dried out.
Maybe even dead.

Hush   listen.
The oak, it whispers stories.
That bloodwood, it sings.
Story song story song.

A wind caresses the trees as it
gathers up stories and songs.
Weaving through the branches
before dispersing song and story.

See. There's new growth on that branch.
Definitely not dead.
Just watching   listening   thinking.
Waiting for knowing. Still here, but

Listen   hush.
That branch hums.
Song   story   song   story.
Whispering story, while their heart sings.

At night, when all is quiet
rivers of song and story flow from the sky.
Tiny stars nestle joyfully on both trees
waiting eagerly for that branch to hum.

Powerful Unconditional
Shania Richards

watched Mum use art like painting
heading to recover from depression
tells me that we're a patient people
that loves to treasure family
shows that we've been through a lot
                together
that we survived the colonial trauma
that we can't afford real jewelry
but we knew how to make it

cried when Mum gave me the gift after we buried her mum
now I carry them everywhere on my throat
we don't have much but Mum made sure I had a voice
to proudly show our spirits
that we carry on our ancestors DNA while country heals

powerful
unconditional
love
knowing

Ruby
Nancy Bates

Ruby made the music come to life
For the love of a woman will give a man a reason to write
When a woman gives her love
It's a gift that lifts a broken man up

Ruby used to strum on her guitar
Searching for a melody or words that would explain away the past
When a woman has known pain
She loves deeper than almost anything

She asks nothing of herself
She'll outplay the tainted cards she's dealt
She has weathered many storms
But through the dark and through the cold
Ruby's heart was always warm

Ruby stood beside him on the stage
Sharing what becomes of love when there's music and a big wide
        world to change
When a woman sings her song, tells her story
It makes every woman strong

Blood-Memory Cultural-Flows
Natalie Harkin

Kumarangk | remember a small island peaceful and slow where the fresh and salt-waters meet. a ferry used to cross these waters. pelicans catch a free ride to stand wise and proud waiting for fish and dreams to catch – until that bridge. how sad the people who cannot slow down to ride with a pelican. lower lakes churn memory toward her wide-open mouth so we taste blood and bone resting deep and shallow while casuarinas sigh sing and cry-up the wind. reeds push through her silty skin to be picked and dried and soaked to weave precious stories of Old Ones. from fish-traps to midden-sites her sand-dunes drift-settle-shift and rest so everywhere a trace of her on tides – from birth-life-death to birth. all past-present-futures pump from the land our brown body. this small island. they said she fabricated her beliefs but we know there is no horizon to the stars and seven sisters never end. we will know her fight for justice and ngatjis and babies and ancestors for as long as it takes. as long as it takes. for a small island. Ngarrindjeri yarluwar-ruwe. known by some as Hindmarsh Island. always Kumarangk. these cultural flows.

Charlotte | every Saturday morning the Tuckwell boys walk a familiar route along the river's edge for fish to buy. the best catch in the district they say. scaled-trimmed-gutted and honoured with care. they cut through town trace a slight rise behind Armfield Slip and stop just before reaching the railway line. Walker's Camp. they call it the outskirts but Old Nanna Charlotte calls it her beating-heart. the last semi-traditional people in Goolwa they say. respected and proud. renowned fishers and weavers and fighters in white wars. her pulgi is rough with iron-sheets and hessian bags on a spread of thorny weeds. inside is beautiful and clean. neat as a pin. come mid-week she delivers her catch across town before landing herself on Old Lady

Tuckwell's deep verandah. they drink hot tea from bone-china. she smokes her pipe. the young Tuckwell boys see her as a grumpy old woman. a mystery pungent with river-gifts. it's 1936. she is eighty-five years witnessing colonial-entitlement and colossal invasion as rapid as the river is wide. townsfolk with pitchforks hunger for prime-land while she sleeps. there is a quiet chill on the darkest new moon as they covertly torch her camp that winter's night. impossible flames. Old Nanna Charlotte fades as river-sorrows churn and rise to meet her plight. her blood-memory grows toward that canoe-tree place where she finally rests. we remember. from womb to womb with the force of time see her glow on the moon and shimmer blackened tides. these cultural flows.

Karra | slow agitations occupy tributaries with dredging and fracking and South-East drains. concrete networks channel fresh flood-plain waters out to sea. we are drought-stricken storm-beaten and flooded with grief. salt-crystals rise with ignorance while domestic taps run putrid in shades of cloudy-to-black. 'Public Notice Boil Water Alerts' are stapled to country-town trees: *Water used for drinking or food preparation should be brought to a rolling boil to make it safe. Children should take bottled water or cool boiled water to school* (Walgett, New South Wales); *Children must avoid swallowing water or getting water up their nose when showering, bathing or playing with water* (Oodnadatta, South Australia); *Boiling the* [arsenic-poisoned] *town water will not make it safe to drink and bottled water should be used for drinking, food preparation, making ice, cleaning teeth and gargling* (Uralla, New South Wales). our sacred Country under siege might best be conjured from the perspective of fish. small spotted and swift or giant Elders of the deep. they glide strong and quiet. carve rivers as stories and stories as rivers to feed and glisten and spawn new life. blue-green algae fully thrives to bloom then die. oxygen levels fall and asphyxiation levels rise. Karra. Old River Red Gums carrying centuries of story lean-in to witness. fish thrash wildly at her roots then chase stagnant shallows toward a slow gentle float. they rest in their millions as layers of riverbank sediment transform to hot dried clay. these mighty trees bearing floodwater stains recognise massacre and drop another limb with the weight of despair. as lifelines give way to a thirsty greedy chain of water-thieving infrastructure our Elders seek reflections of home and weep. they demand – *who will honour the fish?* these cultural flows.

Yartapuulti | small at the wharf's edge. face west across the water to see a $2 billion redevelopment all lit-up in neon satisfaction. this high-rise high-density waterside housing for the rich. this glittering neo-colonial backdrop reflected on her black-night's river. face west across the water to this potent site. Lartelare's birthplace and remnants of home. she is *keeper of the black swans.* Yartapuulti. this river flooded with story carries memory on undercurrents that pull and twist in surprising directions. moments are captured and dragged down to settle with sediment. seep into past-present-future memory. imprint on fine-silted skin. this translucent familiar is like a drop of essence. a spill of blood. a lingering trace as black-swan ripples hold our gaze. as the river swells dive-in to drink it all then dissolve on time luring deep-deeper toward shards of light that slice and glide. a soft sliding fade where sun cannot reach. where surfaces no longer glisten. this is the quietest-dark and never still. search for memories on currents and decades of protest. find flags flying peace and torrent-rage. generations of bloodshed and tears drive the tides so open-up to taste it all. sweet-solidarity reflects new neon-light stories on a dark moon and we are still awake in the land of sleep. we are still afloat on the land of grief. here at this site we remember. we miss our beloved elder-Aunty-wise friend. Aunty Veronica. this float of imaginings flows straight to her heart and together we watch *'campfires lit up all the way to Outer Harbor … just like fairyland'*. no high-rise-neon-light-dreams here. only Lefevre-Peninsula-Love on a quiet drift. these cultural flows.

Cultural flows | we are mangrove and rock-hole and fresh-water spring. we are mighty drifts of brown-green-blue to seep and drain from vein to outlet to river and sea. we rest with midden-sites blue-whale bones sandy-ridges and chenier-plains. we find memories of old ways interrupted and sit with Elders who know how stay awake in this land of sleep. we are inherited responsibility so future generations will know this once-upon-a-time perfectly balanced magnificent web of life. they will know to hold space for lands-waters-spirits-skies. they will know to carry culture and lore and epic beauty forward as whole and fragmented and vibrant and disrupted. we are ocean-life spawning in seagrass blankets. we are tidal marshlands labouring hard to ebb-flow and lure fish and crabs and snails to creeks at high and low-tide. these flows can't be calculated by suits and assessment tools in scientific spreadsheets but are lived and loved between waves of story and blood-memory-honouring. like salt-of-the-earth we rise to settle-unsettle survive and thrive and we refuse to disappear. these our cultural flows.

Originally published in the catalogue *Between Waves* (editor Jessica Clark) as part of the Yalingwa exhibition series, Adelaide Centre for Contemporary Art, Melbourne, July 1–3, 2023.

Contributors

Noah Amundson is Arrernte, born and currently residing on Kaurna Yarta. As a university student, he has developed a keen interest in the fields of environmental science, geography and education. Noah has recently embraced writing as a means of sharing his life experiences. In addition to his academic pursuits, Noah enjoys visiting second-hand stores, appreciating nature, and pursuing photography as a hobby.

Ben Armstrong is an aspiring Wiradjuri writer who uses his love for tabletop game storytelling, fantasy, science fiction and his upbringing to craft unique and character-focused stories. When Ben isn't writing, he is the Head of Gaming at Awesome Black, leading a team creating a video game in an Indigenous futurism setting. Ben has a background in technology and computer science careers of over 20 years.

Nancy Bates is a First Nations composer, writer, educator, and proudly Barkindji. With cultural ties to communities running the length of the Baarka, she is a river woman living a multifaceted life, intertwining music, education, and advocacy to weaponise and resist colonisation. Recognising her exceptional contributions to the music industry, Nancy Bates has been honoured as an Ambassador for the Australasian Performing Right Association.

Edoardo Crismani is a Wiradjuri filmmaker, writer, poet and songwriter. His documentary *The Panther Within*, a tribute to his grandfather, boxer Joe Murray, was nominated for an Australian Writers Guild Award and has regularly been shown on NITV and SBS. Edoardo was awarded a 2023 Boundless Indigenous Writers Mentorship to complete his debut novel under the guidance of Tara

June Winch. He was the coordinator of the South Australian First Nations Writers group 2019–2023.

Brad Darkson (Narungga) is a multidisciplinary artist currently working across various media including carving, video, sound, animation, sculpture, painting and site-specific installation. 'Cultural-revival-activism' permeates his work, focusing on connections between contemporary and traditional cultural practice, language and lore.

Ali Cobby Eckermann is a Yankunytjatjara poet, artist and grandmother residing on Ngadjuri country. Her traditional desert country and family influenced her first collections *little bit long time*, *Kami* and *Inside My Mother*. In later years her poems have been influenced by the sky. The latest release is *She Is The Earth* (Magabala, 2023).

Kathryn Gledhill-Tucker is a Nyungar technologist, writer, digital rights activist living on Whadjuk Noongar boodjar. Their creative practice explores the intersection of activism, science-fiction, and technology in imagining radical futures and ushering them into existence.

Dominic Guerrera (Kaurna, Ngarrindjeri) is a poet, curator and ceramicist. His writings have been published in Artlink and Cordite Review. Guerrera was the recipient of the 2021 Oodgeroo Noonuccal Indigenous Poetry Prize. He is a co-editor of *The Rocks Remain* anthology and the First Nations Literary Editor at Cordite Review.

Natalie Harkin (Narungga) is a poet and academic with a strong interest in archival justice, engaging archival-poetic methods to document community Memory Stories, Aboriginal women's domestic service labour histories, and Indigenous Living-Legacy archive innovations for our time. Her books include *Dirty Words* (Cordite Books), *Archival-poetics* (Vagabond Press), and *APRON-SORROW / SOVEREIGN-TEA* (to be published by Wakefield Press).

Sheena Hayes is a 35-year-old Arrernte woman from Alice Springs, Central Australia. Her hobby is poetry, and she enjoys reading and writing poetry.

Lulu Houdini is a Gamilaroi poet and midwife. Lulu's work explores invisibility, memory, resistance, and liminality. Her work has been published with *Meanjin*, *Overland* and *Red Room Poetry*. Lulu currently creates and lives with Jerrinja Wandi Wandandian Country.

Michael Larkin is a Kokatha poet and academic working at Adelaide University. His poetry has been published through Ginninderra Press (*The Crow*) and Hills Poets Anthology (*Ripples*). Michael's writing stems from deep observation and reflection on the beauty and sorrow of the world. His poetry is both political and philosophical, critiquing power and its influence as a corruptive force.

Tabitha Lean is a criminalised woman using words and stories to challenge the hegemony the colony holds over 'legitimate' knowledge about criminality and those who 'offend' to counter the incessant reproduction of racialised dynamics and white stories favoured and valorised by the literati. Her work seeks to disrupt these canons, and challenge people to think differently about what people can teach us about state violence by changing the way stories are told, and by whom.

Angie Faye Martin (Kooma/Kamilaroi/European) is a writer/editor currently living on Gubbi Gubbi Country (Redcliffe). She worked in public policy for 15 years before launching a freelance editing business, Versed Writings. She has a Bachelor of Public Health, a Masters of Anthropology, and an ever-growing passion for fiction. Her work has appeared in *Meanjin*, *Garland* and the *Saltbush Review*.

Steven Pappin is an Australian Barkindji man. He comes from a background of diverse cultural heritage: French, Scottish, German, Osage (Indigenous American) and Barkindji (Australian Aboriginal). A well-travelled man with life experiences more diverse than his bloodlines, he has done everything from amateur kick-boxing to writing/editing university-level curricula. He is the modern-day proverbial warrior poet.

Dylan Peisley, known as Muldari Ko:rni to his Old People, is a Ngarrindjeri, Boandik, Gunditjmara, Māori ko:rni living and creating on Kaurna Yerta. Interested in holding to ancient ways, Dylan uses words to speak the past into the present to safeguard the future for his mob. Dylan believes this country has a Blak past and future, and works with Aboriginal kids to ensure they not only survive in colonial Australia, but prosper despite the violence of the colony.

Taryn Poole is a Ngarrindjeri and Kaurna mi:mini, born and raised on Kaurna country. She started writing in her teens to express her thoughts and feelings, and create a healing process as she struggled with cultural identity, childhood trauma and mental health. Writing helps her contextualise experiences and build insight to the inner-self and life – a creative source of therapy. Like her grandmother Aunty Margaret Brusnahan, Taryn hopes to continue the tradition of storytelling with contemporary ways of sharing new experiences, understood through Indigenous lenses.

Sonya Rankine is a Ngarrindjeri, Narungga, Ngadjuri and Wirangu woman currently living at Moonta Bay on Narungga Country, Yorke Peninsula. Sonya is an artist, weaver and singer/songwriter. Sonya's art extends to writing poetry which has always been part of her creative expression and strongly linked to her song writing process. Sonya's poetry tells stories of her life experiences, and addresses social and political issues which are strongly interconnected to her life, family and community as an Aboriginal woman.

Shania Richards is a Barngarla, Wirengu, Nao, Mirning, Ndjau, Gubrun, Bulang, Noongar, Wongutha artist working in performing arts, writing, game development and visual arts. Born in Kalgoorlie, and now living on the Eyre Peninsula, Shania has been influenced by her grandfather Neil Dimer, grandmother Janet Beck, and parents Belinda Dimer and Clarence Richards. In 2023 she was Artist of the Month at the Nautilus Art Centre.

Brooke Scobie is a queer, AuDHD, Goorie poet, writer and multi-disciplinary creative living on Darkinjung land. Their work is a love letter to Country and to those marginalised by society, previously featured in publications like *Overland Journal*, *Running Dog*, *Red Room Poetry* and SBS. They were a finalist for the 2023 David Unaipon Award, achieved second in the 2020 Judith Wright Poetry Prize, and have performed at the Sydney Biennale, Melbourne Writers Festival, and Queer Stories.

Rick Slager lives on Karta, an island off the coast of South Australia with his partner, a little black dog and a naughty magpie. Like his ancestors, Rick worked as a professional fisherman. This career gave him a greater opportunity to read, daydream and yarn than most, and it's where he developed a love for story.

Barrina South is a Barkindji artist, poet and critic. In 2023, her short story *Family Tree* was adapted for the stage by the Mill Theatre, Canberra and she was commissioned to write an ekphrastic poem for the National Gallery of Australia. Her work has featured in *Rabbit*, *Authora Australia*, *Cordite Review*, *Kuracca* and *Teesta Review: A Journal of Poetry, India*. Barrina was awarded a 2024 Varuna First Nation fellowship, and her debut collection of poetry is currently in development.

Alexis West has worked as a dancer, choreographer, performer, voice talent, writer, director, producer, researcher, dental assistant, parent, poet, theatre-maker, filmmaker, collaborator. A proud Birri Gubba, Wakka Wakka, South Sea Islander, Caucasian woman living on Kaurna Country. Alexis is passionate about sharing her unique perspectives and observations on belonging, blessings and transgressions.

Jayda Wilson is a proud Gugada and Wirangu emerging artist living and working on unceded Kaurna Yarta. Wilson's current work focuses on the connection between language and identity, as they ground themselves culturally and affirm sovereignty through Gugada and Wirangu wangga, embedded in country in the far west of South Australia. Through working in mediums of sound, print, poetry and photography, Wilson's practice is a journey to reclaiming their mother tongue, celebrating wangga through the re-telling of family history, (re)memory and (re)archiving.

Karen Wyld is an author of Martu descent living on the south coast of Adelaide. Karen's books include *Where the Fruit Falls* (historical novel, University of WA Publishing) and *Heroes Rebels and Innovators* (children's nonfiction, Hachette). Karen is a SA Literary Fellowship 2024 recipient, and co-editor of *The Rocks Remain* anthology.

Wakefield Press is an independent publishing and
distribution company based in Adelaide, South Australia.
We love good stories and publish beautiful books.
To see our full range of books, please visit our website at
www.wakefieldpress.com.au
where all titles are available for purchase.
To keep up with our latest releases, news and events,
subscribe to our newsletter.

Find us!

Facebook: www.facebook.com/wakefield.press
Twitter: www.twitter.com/wakefieldpress
Instagram: www.instagram.com/wakefieldpress